P9-DHR-830
SALTY LAGOON
SCARLETT'S HOUSE
SLINK'S HOLE
SASS AND FRASS'S HOUSE
MULBERRY MARSH
MOONFLOWER MEADOW
FIDDLESTICKS DAM
BLOSSOM'S LODGE
DIXIE'S DEN
MINNOW CREEK
LOBLOLLY POND
PERCY'S HOUSE
GLADE
DUMP

When a hurricane blew through the swampy Everglades, two little eggs were swept from their nests and floated down the river. After the storm was over, the eggs hatched side by side in the soft, sweet grass of the riverbank. And that is how an alligator named Spike and a snowy egret named Mike came to live together as brothers in a very special place known as Cypress Glade.

Save the Swamp

By MARY PACKARD
Illustrations based on characters created
and designed by Lisa McCue

GROLIER ENTERPRISES INC.
DANBURY, CONNECTICUT

Printed in the United States of America. Published by Grolier Direct Marketing, Danbury, Connecticut.
Design by Antler & Baldwin Design Group. ISBN: 0-7172-8307-0
A SPIKE & MIKE™ BOOK PRINTED ON RECYCLED PAPER

It was a bright, sunny morning in Cypress Glade. Dixie Otter was building a big mud hill by the edge of the swimming hole. But she wasn't having much fun. Today was moving day. By this time tomorrow, she and her family would be gone from Cypress Glade.

Spike the alligator and Mike the bird were on their way over to Dixie's house to say good-bye. They were going to miss their playful friend.

"I can't believe Dixie is moving," said Mike.
"I know," agreed Spike. "Things just won't be the same around here without her."

Dixie perked up when she saw Spike and Mike.

"I have to go soon, but we still have a little time to play," she said. "Watch this!"

Spike and Mike watched Dixie slide down the mud hill on her belly. She hit the water with a big splash.

Spike went belly sliding, too, but Mike, who was not too fond of mud, jumped into the water from a vine swing instead.

When Mike came up for air, there was a plastic bag dangling from his beak.

"Yuk!" complained Mike. "This water is not very clean, is it?"

"Not as clean as it used to be," said Dixie.

When the three friends got out of the water, Mr. and Mrs. Otter were waiting for them.

"My feathers feel sticky," said Mike.

"My eyes are burning," complained Spike.

"I'm not surprised," said Mr. Otter. "The water is very dirty."

"Yes," added Mrs. Otter sadly. "That's why we have to move. Dirty water is unhealthy."

"But we're going to miss you so much," said Spike.

Mr. and Mrs. Otter knew that the family had to leave Cypress Glade, even if it meant leaving their friends.

"I'm sorry," said Mr. Otter. "We have no choice. We otters spend so much of our time in the water—it has to be clean or we might get sick!"

So they strapped their suitcases to their backs and began to swim away.

"Bye," called Dixie, waving sadly.

Spike and Mike waved back.

"I wish we could do something," said Spike.

"Let's find Tallulah," said Mike. "Maybe she can help."

Tallulah the turtle was in her garden when Spike and Mike came looking for her.

"Hello, boys," she said. "Why do you look so sad?"

"Dixie Otter moved away today," said Spike.

"That's right," replied Tallulah. "I heard that the Otter family was moving."

"They moved because of the water," said Spike. "It isn't clean enough for them to live here anymore."

"Why don't we have a town meeting?" suggested Tallulah. "I think it's time for us to figure out what to do about our water."

"Great idea," said Mike. "I'll ring the bell."

Mike rang the bell in the tower at Town Hall, and everyone hurried over to see what was going on.

A town meeting meant that something important needed to be discussed. All the animals were curious to find out what it was.

Tallulah told them about the problems with the water, and they all agreed it was time to clean up the swamp.

"We used to be able to see clear to the bottom," said Scarlett the flamingo.

"And the plants that grow along the edge of the swamp are starting to wilt and turn brown," added Blossom the beaver.

"It looks like we have a lot of work to do," said Spike. "Let's get started."

Meanwhile, the otters had moved to their new home in Marigold Marsh. It was very pretty, but it was very far from Cypress Glade. In fact, it was very far from any town at all.

"I'm so lonely," said Dixie sadly.

"Don't worry," said Mrs. Otter. "We will look for the other otters. Soon you will have friends to play with. You'll see."

Back in Cypress Glade everyone pitched in to clean up the water. The frog brothers Gumbo and Jumbo dived to the bottom of the swimming hole. When they came up, their arms were filled with plastic knives and forks and plates and cups.

"These must be from picnics we've had here," said Gumbo.

"Too bad we weren't more careful," said Jumbo.

Two raccoons named Sass and Frass swam around and collected plastic bags and candy wrappers that were floating in the water.

"The next time I have a candy bar, I'll be sure to throw the wrapper where it belongs," said Sass.

"Me, too," agreed Frass.

Scarlett worked harder than she had ever worked before.

"I can't believe how messy some of my neighbors are!" she exclaimed. "I always throw my things in the trash."

"Always?" repeated Mike, holding up a used paint brush he'd just found floating in the water. "This used to be yours, didn't it?"

"Yes," admitted Scarlett, blushing to an even deeper shade of pink. "I guess I'm not as careful as I thought I was."

Scarlett wasn't the only one who had been careless. As the friends worked, they all found things in the water that they had thoughtlessly tossed aside.

When all the trash had been gathered, everyone helped pile it into wagons and wheelbarrows. Then they hauled it off to the dump.

"Put the stuff right here," said Percy the pack rat, who was always glad to get more junk. Then he got busy sorting and placing it in the proper recycling bins.

The next day everyone helped cut back the old, wilted plants so they could grow healthy and strong again.

When they were finished with the big cleanup, Spike noticed that the water still didn't look too clean.

"Wait until it rains a few times," Tallulah told him.

And sure enough, after several weeks and a few rainstorms, the water began to look much better. The plants perked up and the flowers bloomed.

"We did a good job, didn't we?" asked Mike, admiring the sweet-smelling flowers. "Don't you wish that Mr. and Mrs. Otter could see their home now?"

"I do, indeed," replied Tallulah. "In fact, I think it's time to find the otters and ask them to come back to Cypress Glade.

"That's a great idea! I'll look for them," said Mike.

Mike searched and searched. He flew over Moonflower Hill, Cattail Creek, and Mossy Bog. He got all the way to Marigold Marsh before he finally spotted the otters.

"There they are!" he said to himself.

"I have the best news!" he told the surprised otter family. "After you left, we all worked and worked to make the water clean again. Won't you please come back and see for yourselves?"

"Could we?" begged Dixie.

Mr. Otter looked at Mrs. Otter.

"All right," she said. "We miss our old home, too."

The otters packed their things and started the long swim home. Mike flew back to spread the good news.

Then everyone got busy. They scrubbed and scrubbed the otters' old house until it was gleaming. To decorate the house, they brought in a big bouquet of wild flowers. They even made a big "Welcome Home" sign.

"Can we go play now?" asked Dixie.
"Go ahead," said Mrs. Otter. "It sure is good to be home!"

Let's Talk About It

The water in Cypress Glade had become too dirty to use. It was polluted. So, at a town meeting, Spike and Mike and all their friends decided to work together to make the water clean again.

Imagine if everyone in the world joined together to solve the problem of water pollution. In fact, leaders from many countries are trying to make this happen. They have met, and plan to meet again, to talk about ways to clean up the waters around the world.

You don't have to be a world leader to do something about water pollution. Fourteen-year-old Kevin Bell noticed that the birds and fish in the wetlands near his home in Nevada were dying. So he started a group that worked to replace the dirty water with clean water.

For people who do not live near wetlands, rivers, ponds, or streams, there is another way to protect the water. Did you know that if you dig deep enough, you will find water underground? Many people depend on this water for drinking. Because the earth acts like a big sponge that soaks up anything that falls on it, we all have to be careful not to spill anything harmful on the ground. For example, a small amount of paint or motor oil can damage many gallons of groundwater.

Maybe you and some of your friends would like to work together to clean up the waters in your area. Be sure to ask an adult to help you. If we all pitch in to help, our water will be fresh and clean for everyone to enjoy.

Welcome Home

When Dixie and her parents got back to Cypress Glade, everyone was waiting for them.

"Look how clean the water is!" cried Dixie.

"That's right," agreed Spike. "And we learned that it's a lot easier not to dump things in the water than it is to clean it up later!"

Where Do They Live?

Look at the pictures below. Point to the four animals that live in the water. Point to the four animals that live on land. Now point to the four animals that spend part of their time in the water and part of their time on land. All of these animals need clean water to live.

water dwellers: octopus, fish, whale, lobster
land dwellers: cat, cow, chicken, giraffe
both: frog, salamander, walrus, seal

← MANGROVE MARSH
SUGARBERRY MARSH
TALLULAH'S HOUSE
SPIKE
BO'S BURROW
TO ← TOWN
N
W
E
S
SPIKE AND MIKE'S BIG OLD CYPRESS TREE
GUMBO AND JUMBO'S HOUSE
CYPRESS